Winter's
Cold Kiss

Michael Young

ROYAL MEDIA
PUBLISHING

Royal Media and Publishing
Jeffersonville, IN 47131
http://royalmediaandpublishing.com
royalmediapublishing@gmail.com

Cover Design: Elite Covers

ISBN-13: 978-1-955501-25-5

Printed in the United States of America

Dedication

To everybody that has ever enjoyed a book.

ROYAL MEDIA
PUBLISHING

Table of Contents

Prologue

Flashes of flames from a handgun popped up in the night like giant red fireflies, along with ringing, echoing sounds of bullets bouncing off metal and concrete. Shadows scrambled to hide behind anything large enough. The bullets no longer came in random bursts, but in single precise shots. Every time the outline of a head peeked over or around an object, a flash was seen and the sparks from a bullet caused the head to retreat.

"You son-of-a-bitch! You're going to run out of ammo sooner or later, and that ass is good as dead. Believe that, shit man!"

Then, another spark caused the man to fall back down on the ground behind a dumpster. His partner looked through the window of a parked car to see where their target was. As he scanned the night streets, a brick came flying from around a tree and caused the only street light around to explode, sending everything into complete darkness.

"What are you waiting on? You saw where that shit just came from! Blast that fool!" the guy by the car yelled.

Before the guy by the dumpster could raise his gun and aim in the direction from where the brick was thrown, sounds of hurried footsteps in the dark made it seem like they were all around them. He fired anyway, hitting a tree and a fire hydrant.

"You should have fired when I said so, mother—"

Before he could finish the insult, the window of the car he was hiding behind blew out from a bullet, showering him with glass. Then two more hit the hood of the car, followed by more footsteps and the clang of metal hitting the ground. He thought to himself, *about time he's out of bullets.*

"Yo, Wildout, you alright?"

"Covered in glass now, but I'm good. Where he at, Bulldog?"

"It's too damn dark. I can't see shit. I think he ran down the street. Cover me, man, I'm going after him." Then he spun around from behind the dumpster and ran for maybe five feet before he was blown backwards by a single shot— direct shot to the head, right through the left eye.

"Bulldog! Bulldog!" Wildout yelled to his assassin partner. As he looked under the car, he saw his guy flat out on the ground with his head pointed towards him. He couldn't see his face in the dark, but he knew Bulldog was dead.

The shooter never said a word through the whole chase and shootout. He just let his gun speak for him. After the body fell, he took off in a full sprint into the night air, knowing no one would be following him the rest of this night.

Chapter One

Steam fogged up the glass shower door in a beautiful, marble-accented bathroom. As the water was turned off and a cloud of steam filled the room, sunlight illuminated the silhouette of a shapely figure stepping out of the shower. A towel was thrown from the cloud and a woman emerged like a goddess coming from Mount Olympus. She paused in front of the mirror to dry her hair. Coming out of the bathroom and into the joined bedroom, she stopped in the doorway.

"Hey, sleepy head, you going to lie there all morning?"

The body lying in the king-sized bed with the gold velvet and satin sheets began to stir. "Just let me get another fifteen minutes. I promise I'll get up then."

The woman in the doorway shifted her stance. "Are you sure? In ten minutes, all this will be downstairs, eating and about to start my day."

The sheets came down off his face and his head raised slightly. "Fifteen, I promise..."He stopped mid-sentence. His attention was no longer on getting more sleep. "Oh, my damn!" he said, sitting up more in the bed.

The woman stood in the doorway. She put her hands up on the upper corner of the doorway, separating her legs. Now, with the steam evaporated out of the bathroom, the sunlight coming through the window from behind made her look like a goddess from the heavens.

The man in the bed sat up and let his right leg drop to the floor. He scanned the woman like a red beam on a bar code. She didn't have the world's definition of perfection, but she was his. Every curve and shape was that of his ideal woman. Anytime her body changed, his idea of a perfect woman changed with her. By the time his eyes had moved down to the beads of water running down her calves, the sheets were up in tent-form right where his lap was.

"Well, Mr. Topp. Either you have a ruler standing under those sheets, or you see something you like." Then she shook her hair out, making it hug her face and cover one eye. Her hair was so unique, it looked blue on most days, and this was one of those days.

"Mrs. Topp, you know how that look turns me on." Just like a dog wags its tail in excitement, he began to wag his penis under the sheets, which he knew turned her on.

She casually strolled over to the bed as her husband slid to the middle, eagerly waiting for his wife. Crawling onto the bed, she lay on top of him and softly kissed him.

"Winter! How in the hell did I get so lucky to have you enter my life?"

"I guess it was something that was meant to be, Stephon. Right now, I want you to give me that reason those covers were up in that tent."

Stephon wrapped his arms around her waist to position his wife correctly, then inserted his long, hard muscle inside her and made slow love.

Chapter Two

Wildout drove his SUV up to a basic, plain-looking house set back from the other homes that surrounded it. The house was nice, but nothing stood out about it. In fact, the luxury SUV that now sat in front of it looked out of place. He got out and walked to the front door, hanging his head. Bulldog wasn't his best friend, but he was a cool ass dude to hang with. However, this wasn't the reason his head was down. He knew that coming back unsuccessful was going to be trouble.

Before he could ring the doorbell, a voice came from an unseen speaker. "Don't bother with the bell. The door is open." Wildout knew the voice from the speaker; it was Big Joe. He was basically the doorman and look-out.

Now inside, he looked around to see who was in the first room. A few low-level flunkies, playing video games on a 47" television, a small Bluetooth iPod dock in the corner bumping some new hip-hop rapper. Walking past them, he glanced into the one bedroom. Big Joe was there, sitting in a large lazy-boy chair watching several small screens on top of an old floor model set. He nodded 'what up' to Big Joe, who just glared back at him for a response.

Before entering the kitchen, he heard Big Joe say, "That fucking ride cost crazy coins, man."

"I know, man, I know!"

The kitchen was filled with the smell of a wonderful meal. Whatever it was, had already been served and eaten. There were two doors in the back of the kitchen. One went to the basement and the other was an empty closet.

Wildout yelled back over his shoulder, "Yo, Joe!" Then a secret door opened in the back of the closet. He entered and took an elevator down inside the wall, going deeper than the basement. When the door opened, he stepped into a layer that was bigger than the house itself. White tile mixed with white carpet on the floor. Art work lined the walls. Nothing valuable, just nice paintings by local artists. Several nice theater-style chairs were arranged around the room, with an oversized leather swivel chair set in front of them.

Wildout sat in the back of the room. "Oh no, Wildout, bring your ass down front!" a deep voice called out.

As he sat down, he looked around to see who was there. Tyler, known as Dragon, a fellow get-it-done guy like himself and Bulldog. Cedric, better known as Serpent, a really grimy dude. He would rob a kid if he knew his pockets were stuffed. Cano, a.k.a Volcano, a true hothead. A guy who was down and ready to get into some trouble at any time and sometimes would start some, just to have something to do. Then there was the guy at the right hand of the boss...

"Where is Bulldog, Wildout? " the voice asked from the large chair in front of everyone.

"He caught a hot one and didn't make it."

"What about the target?"

"After he took Bulldog, he got ghost."

"Why didn't you tombstone him before or after that?"

"He shot out a window and put glass in my eyes, so I—"

"Well, that explains the after, but what about before he killed Bulldog? There was two of y'all and didn't both of you guys have guns?"

"Yes, sir. See, these big-butt freaks were all over us—"

"Ah shit!" Serpent said, shifting in his chair.

"Big-butt freaks, you say?" Then the chair spun around. Now facing Wildout, was Adrianos, better known as Adonis. Adonis was true to his namesake. At least 6′ 8″ and around 320 pounds of hulking muscle. He wasn't in bodybuilder shape, more like very built football player. "Big butt... what the fuck do you have on?"

"What, this suit? I had it tailored."

"You know the rules. We don't look expensive, so we don't draw attention to our business. First, your stupid ass buys that Maserati SUV, now tailored suits!"

Adonis sat in his leather seat, wearing a simple jogging suit bought from Burlington and some old, worn-out Air Jordans. He also drove a 2000 something Ford Explorer. Although it had a 500 horsepower Roush motor, you couldn't tell by the look of it. The whole crew dressed like any normal person on the street just trying to make it.

Wildout was about to try to plead his case when Adonis called out a name, "Bezerk! Game time!" From his side, out of the shadows, a man stepped with a pearl white gun in hand. The gun went *boom*, and the middle of Wildout and the back of his chair exploded. Bezerk smiled from the time he emerged until the body slid out of the chair.

"I want that motherfucker, Zerk!"

"Dead, or alive so you can lay hands, boss?"

"Dead! Oh... and dealer's choice. Any way you want to do it." Adonis knew Bezerk would not fail him.

"Dragon, Serpent, get that shit out of the driveway and turn it to Lego blocks."

The men all got up and left the room to do their jobs. Adonis spun back around in his chair to look at a picture on his cellphone. "You'll never get to sing your song to anyone, little canary!" Then he crushed a full, unopened can of beer that he had been about to drink.

Chapter Three

———— ⚜ ⚜ ————

Winter lay in bed on her side as she watched her husband get dressed for work. She knew the sex they'd just had was only an appetizer to the main event later that night. Most nights when Stephon got home, he was so drained that he would fall asleep right after dinner. She wasn't exactly sure what he did, but the pay was outstanding and the benefits were plentiful. The drawback was her husband being worn out completely, like last night. When he got home, all he did was sit next to her on the couch and fall asleep. Although he did try to talk for a little while, Stephon couldn't even eat before he was in bed snoring.

"Babe, why do they have you coming back in so soon? You got home so late last night and were so tired."

"I know, hon. I came across some information that my bosses need to hear about."

"Couldn't it wait for a few more hours? Shit! It's not like it's a matter of life and death!" She gave him a halfhearted smile that slowly changed.

Stephon turned to face his wife with a tombstone look. "It is."

She sat up and looked back at him, surprised. "What do you mean by it is?"

Knowing his wife sometimes questioned his faithfulness and wondered what he really did, after the close call last night—the closest ever, he decided to come clean. "Baby, you need to know what I do. What I really do for a living. I have an office, but my work is mostly in the field. From time to time, I have to—"

There was a loud crashing sound coming from downstairs, like something big just broke. Stephon told his wife to stay in the room while he went to check out the sound. He opened his briefcase that sat on the dresser and pulled out a gun, loaded it and chambered a bullet. As he went to open the door, it flew open and gunshots let loose in the room. The mirror on the wall and several pictures exploded. A lamp was cut in half, and chunks of a wall were taken out.

Stephon hit the floor as soon as the door opened. He caught a bullet in the shoulder and two in the hip. With gun still in hand, he raised it and returned fire. Some thug wanna-be who ran into the room, shooting and not aiming, was hit right under the left eye and dropped at Stephon's feet. Four more shots kept any other fools outside the doorway.

"Winter! Winter, are you okay? Winter!" He moved his head around and saw his wife slumped over a chair in the corner of the room, with blood dripping from her head.

He yelled her name again, then a shotgun blast was heard and the hand he was holding the gun in disintegrated off his arm. He howled in pain as he put the bloody nub under his chest. Looking at his wife's body, he tried to crawl to it.

Laughter was heard as a man holding a smoking double barrel shotgun came in, followed by two more younger guys.

"See, kiddies. That's why you don't rush into a room not knowing the temperature. As you can see, everything is frosty cool now. Hello, Sheldon, or should I say Stephon?"

Stephon looked over his side through watery eyes. There was nothing he could say because he was caught off guard and surprised he was found out. How was his cover blown? How did they find out where he lived? Was Winter all right?

The young guys started taunting him with their tough-guy talk. Bezerk pushed past both of them and pointed the gun at Stephon's left foot, then pulled the trigger. Next, he moved up to his right thigh and squeezed the trigger again. Stephon screamed out in utter pain.

"Damn, Bezerk! That shit is ruthless! Why not just end him?" one of the young ones said, stunned.

"I want this motherfucker to go to Hell in as much pain as possible."

The other young gunner asked, "Yo, man. What did he do?"

Giving both young guys a piercing glare, he said, "He's catching the fury of Adonis. Well, an extension of it, through my hand. Better me than him."

Bezerk then put a foot on Stephon's chest and placed the barrel in his mouth. He shoved it deep down his throat, causing him to choke on his own blood. Seeing that the man was seconds from dying, he removed the barrel and smiled.

BOOM!!! Stephon's head exploded into jelly.

"What about his bitch over there? She thick as fuck. Let's get some pics of that body before we bounce. I need some mental stimulation on those solo nights."

As the guy was walking over to Winter's slumped, bleeding body, Bezerk swung the shotgun and knocked the phone out of his hand, breaking it. "Pick that shit up and get the fuck out of here, before I tell Adonis you wouldn't listen to orders."

The man looked at Bezerk, then the body. Doing as told, he picked up his broken phone and left the room. Looking over his shoulder, Bezerk took one last look at his handiwork and walked out with gun over shoulder.

Chapter Four

There were muffled sounds of people speaking and the sounds of different things beeping. Skin was cold. Ice cold. Then one spot on her arm felt warm, followed by a tap, then another and another. The taps were wet. Winter opened her eyes, and the light in the room caused her head to pound like it was a big drum in a marching band. Standing next to her, crying, was her sister-in-law, Grace Manley.

Winter shifted herself, trying to get more comfortable. "Grace... Grace, where am I?"

Grace's head popped up and her watery eyes widened. "You're finally awake! Doctor! Doctor! She is awake. She is finally awake now. Doctor, nurse!"

The doctor and nurse came in one after the other and checked the equipment around the bed and Winter's vitals. After a brief few minutes, they said that Winter would be just fine in a couple days.

"Grace, what happened? Why am I in the hospital? Where is Stephon? "

"Try to calm down, dear. You're in the hospital. You are suffering from a concussion and several deep cuts. That heavy picture in the bedroom was broken and part of it hit you in the head. The glass from it cut you up pretty good too."

"Okay, I sort of remember something hitting my head. Where is Stephon? We heard a noise, then my memory is foggy."

Grace began to tear up again as she held Winter's hand. "Stephon is gone, honey. He is dead."

Winter jerked her hand away and let anger towards her sister-in-law take control. "You are lying. Where is your damn brother, Grace?" As the anger filled her, the images of the door bursting open and the flashes from guns came back to her memory. Her tone softened again as she asked, "Where is my husband? I need him."

The door to the room opened and a man stepped In. Rob Manely, husband to Grace, and Stephon's co-worker. "I'm sorry, Winter, but he is gone. Down at headquarters, we believe it was a hit."

"A hit? What the hell you talking about? I thought you two were programmers? Who would put a hit on him for that?"

Rob came and stood behind Grace, who was looking at him just like Winter. He told them both that they were not programmers. In fact, they were contracted by the government to infiltrate criminal organizations, to gather information to bring them down. Be it digital or video evidence, anything that would help in the arrest, due to their training from the military for covert operations.

Grace stood up and looked at her husband with surprise. "Rob, how long have you been doing this?"

"For about ten years now. We have an excellent conviction rate. We've taken down at least sixteen major crime factions."

Winter sat speechless, just looking at Rob.

"I'm so sorry, Winter. Stephon was in real deep with this case. We believe they figured out he wasn't who he said he was and followed him home."

"I can't believe he lied to me for so long."

Rob put his hand on her shoulder. "He had to. To protect you."

Grace spoke up. "How much protection was he given? How do they protect you?"

"We're on our own, part of the assignment. Take whatever precautions necessary."

"I guess that didn't work for us, did it?" The anger returned to Winter's voice. "Will the government go ahead and arrest these men?"

"I'm sorry, but I was told that since his cover was blown, the operation is over."

Both women said in unison, "Over?"

Grace asked if they would now get away with murder, and Rob said, "Yes. That is until they can get another person in, get admittance of what they did.

But with how violent and vicious this crew is, getting someone else inside would be damn near impossible."

Winter lay over in her hospital bed, away from Rob and Grace. *If the person they worked for won't do anything, I will do it my fucking self, and no one will be arrested. Death is coming by the coldest Winter anyone has seen.*

Chapter Five

———※ ※———

Three months after the break in, death and funeral of her husband Stephon, Winter sat in their home. A home that felt empty and cold. Cold, like her heart now was. All she could do was think of revenge, but on whom? Rob didn't tell her much about this crime gang they were infiltrating. He and Grace were very comforting, coming by to check on her but giving her enough space to grieve and heal. Which she had totally done except for a few marks on her back and thighs left by the broken, sharp pieces of glass.

She was sitting in a chair in the dark, looking into nothingness, when the doorbell rang. She didn't want company, not this evening. When the bell ringing, she got up, expecting to see Rob or Grace, or maybe even her best friend Mykale. But when she opened the door, a short, balding man stood just off to the side.

"Hello, Winter. How are you holding up, my dear?"

"Doran. Hello. I'm doing. Please come in."

Doran was Stephon and Rob's boss. She had only met him a handful of times. He had called her the first day she got home. He told her if she needed or wanted anything, don't try to contact Stephen's job, call him directly. She wasn't hurting for money because of the insurance policy Stephon had on himself, in addition to the savings they shared. Winter also had money in the bank from a trust fund that her parents had set up for her. With good financial and investing tips from Mykale, she had well over six figures. Stephon never once asked her how much she had. He always said that it was her personal disaster fund and their savings was a storm fund.

"Winter, I won't take up more of your time than I have to. I'm doing something I never thought I would have to do, but here I am."

She sat on the couch, puzzled, while he just stood. Laying a brief case on the coffee table, he took a deep breath. "I was given personal direction to bring you this, in case something ever happened to Stephon, if he didn't make it home. Sorry to say, he won't be coming home." Showing genuine care and concern in his eyes, he continued. "No one knew of this case but me and him. Rob doesn't even know about it. Hell, I don't even know what's in it."

"Really?" Then she looked at the case, her mind working to guess what was in it.

Doran went through his phone and found the combination code. As he read it to Winter, she entered it and the case opened. Inside, was around $500,000 in hundred-dollar bills and a metallic, dark-blue, high-caliber hand gun, with chrome-coated bullets and three clips. Doran looked at the open case and parted his lips but didn't speak.

Winter picked up the gun, inserted the bullets in the clip and loaded the gun in less than thirty seconds.

Doran said, "Question answered," before asked. He touched her shoulder and reminded her of his offer. She nodded then put her attention back to the case. She looked back up and said, "Doran—"

"On the street, they are called Wild Kingdom. The leader's name is The Beast Master, but I believe he is also known as Adonis. BE CAREFUL!"

"Thank you."

He then left, not looking at her again.

Kissing the gun, Winter said to the empty room, "Time for revenge. Winter is coming, and she's going to be a cold bitch!"

Chapter Six

Winter sat in a brand new, high-end SUV, parked in a corner parking lot. She took notice of everyone moving around the block. The obvious dealers stood out to her like candlelight in the dark. The back-and-forth movements in a 10 ft radius, the sleight of hand in the passing of money for product. Dark clothes and hoodies. Stephon had shown Winter the type of guy to look out for when she was out in the world—the shady, thug-hustler type. They would rob you, hurt you and possibly rape you. She was told to be vigilant and careful around these types.

A car pulled up and parked on the opposite corner. The car was old but clean. It sat there for a minute, then a man got out when another man came around the corner. Winter let her tinted window down, to get a better view. The guy walking up was a typical stereotype. Tons of gold and flashy clothes. The man in the car got out and met the guy on the sidewalk. The one in the car looked like everyone else walking around. Sweatpants, Nike shoes and an NFL team jacket. It was barely audible from her distance, but it sounded like he was mad at the man. He pointed out his clothing, then threw a book bag at him.

Winter took mental note of the two men then drove away. She went to several known dope corners around town and saw the same type of dealer everywhere. Also, the same type of street boss.

Flashy, like pimps. Guys who wanted to be known as ballers.

"Damn! How the hell am I supposed to find out which crew killed Stephon? " Winter said to herself. With windows cracked, a voice caught her attention.

"That motherfucker Snowman is going to fuck up the spot and get everyone around here burnt. Don't he know that type of flaunting gets you noticed by the polyester patrol? Dragon said he told him to get rid of that shit and calm it the fuck down."

"I know, man. Glad we were schooled to keep it on the low. Be nice with it, but don't stand out."

"Like that fool Wildout and that expensive ass ride, tailor-made clothes and big fucking diamonds."

"Yeah. Lucky Bezerk didn't do worse to that ass. You heard what he did to that dude and his wife?"

"That was some sick shit I heard. Yo, man, look at that thick bitch over there. She can get the business. I'm 'bout to go claim that fat ass."

"Slow down, man, here comes Dragon."

Bingo, Winter thought. Then she saw the same nice, old-school pull up as before. The two men talking by her ride went over and slapped hands with the man. Dragon, they called him. They all got in the car and left.

Winter pointed at the car from inside her SUV and said, "Now, I have a starting point. Dragon, then find this Bezerk!"

Chapter Seven

———— ⚬ ⚬ ————

After deciding how to approach the street thug, Winter got herself ready. A few days after sitting around possible dope corners, she got lucky and overheard some names and saw some faces. Not knowing how many guys were associated with this Wild Kingdom, she waited to see if the same guys she had seen before came around again. One thing for sure was at least one of them had a thing for thick women. Flipping her hair, she said to herself, "I got that covered."

After about an hour or two, one of the men showed up. He parked a nice looking, basic truck on a corner a block away. Looking at the man, she noticed he wasn't dressed like a baller or a dealer, either. Just another face, a man in the crowd. No sagging pants. No neck full of diamonds and gold. Probably a basic timepiece. No wonder they were hard to find. *Nothing stands out or draws attention to him at all,* she thought.

"Snowman! What up, playa?" He motioned for another man to come over and meet him. As he did, they both walked together.

Winter got out of her vehicle and walked a couple paces behind them, talking to no one on her phone, with ear buds in her ears.

"Snowman, I thought I told you to get this shit corrected?"

"What you talking about, Dragon? The money is on point and the product is moving."

"Not the paper, motherfucker. All this flash you doing. You going to get the spotlight put on you, and I know your bitch ass will sing to the law. Then that would be bad for everybody. Mainly, you, cause then you will have to be fired from life and we would lose a street boy."

"Man, ain't no boy here. What's the need in getting money if you can't look like you're getting money, nigg—"

Dragon stopped to turn and get in his face. "You'd better not finish that. Told you, ain't no niggas in this crew. None! From top of the food chain down to y'all bottom feeders."

By that time, the two guys Winter had heard talking by her ride came up from down the street. They were dressed just like Dragon. Just more normal dudes in a crowd. They slapped hands with Dragon and looked Snowman up and down, then shook their heads. Dragon lit up something and started blowing out big smoke. *Guess that's why he is called Dragon.* Winter paced back and forth, pretending she was arguing with someone. That way, it wouldn't seem like she was listening to the four guys but, eventually, would get noticed.

"Yo, yo, hold up. Not to get off subject, but do y'all see that fine thickness over there by the hydrant?"

Snowman was the first to walk over and try to flaunt and impress. "What up, ma? Why don't you hit the end button on that kid and let a real man satisfy all this thickness?"

Winter kept talking to no one as she turned her back and took a few steps away. Walking backwards, Snowman cursed her out, trying to erase his embarrassment. The two guys burst out in laughter at him when he came back. Dragon just blew smoke in his face and told him, "Told you all that flash only gets you noticed by the police and nothing ass chicks."

"She's just a bitch, that's all," Snowman said as he adjusted his chains.

Taking her buds out, Winter replied, "I'm not a bitch, for your information. I have my own, and looking at your appearance, I have more than you."

The two young guys damn near fell over each other laughing. With his pride thoroughly destroyed, he moved quickly over to her and open-hand slapped her in the face. "You feeling like a bitch now?"

Winter stumbled back, holding her face. She almost reacted, but that would have put her plan in the trash. Luckily, Dragon made a move for her. "That shit right there! Hyenas, go have a talk with Snowman while I see about this young lady." The

two men nodded and guided him behind a building... .
for a talk!

"Sorry about that, honey, you good?" he asked as
smoke left his mouth with every word.

"Yeah, I'm good."

"You won't have to worry 'bout him doing that
again." Before he walked away, he said, "Come by
The Silver Spoon. I would like to officially apologize
for my... uh... friend's actions."

"Okay, sure. I'm not sure when I can make it."

"That's cool. I'll drop a word with them so they can
expect you whenever. What's your name, girly?"

"Winter."

He looked her up and down, then took another pull
of his blunt. "Winter, huh? Okay." Then he winked
and went behind the building with the other three
men.

***

Snowman lay on the ground, beaten up and bloody.
The Hyenas had worked him over good.

"I told you too many times to lose the flash. Didn't
listen. Then you hit a woman who wasn't part of the
Zoo pride. Someone who could have called the
police, and yada-yada. We already had this
conversation."

Before Snowman could protest, Dragon pulled out a gun with a silencer and put three bullets in his head. Unscrewing the silencer, he inhaled the smoke.

"Damn, boss! Why three shots?"

"That's how many times he pissed me off. Ya'll go on and continue to check on everyone, I have to go by The Spoon, then tell Adonis about this fuck and hope I don't end up the same way."

Chapter Eight

———⸎ ⸎———

Winter sat in her home, writing on a pad with a pencil. The doorbell rang and caused her to jump slightly. It wasn't late, but the sun was going down. She didn't get up right away. Instead, she looked at the coffee table in front of her. With the pad and pencil, sat a chrome blue handgun with clips, a small HD mini camera and a pump action assault shotgun. Also, there was a cluster of small daggers with metallic pink blades.

Once again, the bell rang. Winter got up and went to the door. After looking through the peephole and recognizing the person outside, she opened the door and stepped back.

"Hey, girl. Haven't heard from you in a minute so I came by to—"

Seeing the arsenal on the table, Grace stopped mid-sentence. Turning to look at Winter, she stood with her mouth wide open and eyes big.

"What the... what the fuck is all this, Winter? What the hell are you up to?"

Taking a deep breath, Winter motioned for her friend to take a seat. Grace followed her hand but didn't sit near the coffee table. Instead, she sat in a chair across the room.

"You want something to drink?"

Looking at Winter, then at the table and back up, Grace answered, "If you got something with a strong proof, I'll take that. I'm going to need it to listen to this shit!"

Winter poured a drink for each one of them then sat across from her sister-in-law. As she told Grace of her plan, her friend took a bigger swallow after each insane detail of the plan.

"This sounds like some movie shit! How in the hell do you think you're going to pull any of that off?"

"Trust me. I am more than capable of pulling it off."

"What about all this on the table? You carry lipstick and perfume in your bag, not guns. Do you even know how to use that damn thing?"

"Yes, Grace. I know how to use not only this gun, but several assault rifles, shotguns, pump action military grade. Also, I'm pretty good at hand-to-hand combat."

Eyes wide and her cup paused at her mouth, Grace just stared for a second. "How do you know—"

Cutting her off, Winter said, " Stephon! He taught me all this over the years. I never really wanted to learn any of it, but he insisted. Said it never hurts to be prepared for any situation. Just because you don't think it will happen, doesn't mean it never will."

Not sure how much Rob had ever told her about his real work other than what he'd said that day in the hospital, Winter didn't tell Grace what she'd found out about Stephon's death as an undercover agent. It wasn't her place to tell anything dealing with the Manely household. She also didn't mention Doran coming by with a briefcase and more information.

Chapter Nine

After a stunned and amazed Grace left for home, Winter packed everything that was laid out on the table for operation Cold Kiss. She went into the bathroom and turned on the shower so it would be hot and steamy when she was ready to get in. Going into the bedroom next, she called out "play midnight mix". A song came on, playing a nice, mellow slow song. Winter ran her fingers through her hair, rocking her hips to the thumping beat of the music. Removing her clothes like a professional stripper, she made her way to the shower.

Winter sang along with the music as she lathered herself up. With every hot droplet of water on her body, she felt a tiny bit of stress wash off her body. Using the detachable shower head, the water turned to massaging hands. Then the song Stephon used to sing to her came on. In no means, could he carry a tune, but the effort and theatrics he put into it made it enjoyable all the same.

Letting the water flow through her black-blue hair, her mind took over. The water caressed her skin like Stephon used to. It followed her curves like his fingers did. When he did so, her blood would warm, following his fingertips. Stephon didn't have to pay special attention to her natural erotica zones. He created new ones. When they took showers together and he would wash her thighs, his breath on the small part of her spine caused her toes to twist. Then the tender nibble on the ass cheek would make her knees buckle.

With her mind in a heavenly fog, the warm stream that flowed over her breasts felt like Stephon's lips. Opening her eyes, Winter could now see her husband in the steam. The hot water touched her, teased her, loved her, until a thick, sticky nectar mixed with water and soap flowed down between her thighs.

Relaxed and satisfied, Winter dried and put on a silk nightgown. As soon as she got under the covers, old mister sleep was pulling her under. Before she drifted off, she said quietly to the empty room, "Pay back will be a cold bitch!"

Chapter Ten

Dragon, a.k.a Tyler, sat in a large chair across from Serpent, a.k.a Cedric, Volcano, a.k.a Cano, and Jackal, a.k.a Jon. Adonis sat in the back of the room in a chair, on a platform like a throne. Being the unpredictable hothead he was, Bezerk paced the room like a tiger with an empty stomach watching prey.

"So, now that Snowman isn't part of the pride anymore, who is going to take over his field?"

Serpent spoke up and said, "I got enough young vipers out there full of venom. I could handle that no problem."

Volcano then spoke out, saying, "Bullshit. Them young boys are always late paying you and they're lazy as fuck! So how in the hell you going to handle more land when you barely scavenging where you at now?"

"Wouldn't even be an issue if Snowman didn't get taken out."

"Jackal, you need to shut the fuck up. You don't even have territory to claim. We just letting you clean up the scraps from the change having pill heads taking refuge on our land." Serpent said, throwing an empty beer can in his direction.

"Just saying. We don't know the whole story why he's dead. Just the smoke Dragon is blowing up our ass!" Then he side-eyed Dragon.

From his blind side, Bezerk punched Jackal in the mouth, knocking him off his stool. "You were told to shut the fuck up. Keep running your mouth, I'll make sure you won't open it again."

Dragon took a pull of the blunt he was smoking and blew the exhaust towards Jackal and just looked at him.

"You know he was half right. How do we know he busted some chick out in the streets?" Blowing more smoke, "And!"

Then Adonis answered, "He was coming up short. Product going out wasn't matching the paper coming in. So either he was keeping the money, or his team was keeping it from him. Either way, Snowman was responsible. Bottom line, Snowman had to meet that heat."

Serpent looked at Bezerk and asked him, "When have you known Dragon to lie? He may do some stupid high shit, but lying is one thing he don't do."

Looking over at Dragon, Bezerk nodded his agreement then went and sat down in a dark corner. If no one saw him go over there, you would never have known he was there.

"Dragon, do you have any soldiers ready to step up?"

"I'm sure most of them want a chance to eat a bigger portion, but give me a day and I'll find a stand out. Then if he can't handle it, he'll feel my fire."

Adonis tented his fingers and said, "Excellent."

After the meeting, Adonis called Bezerk over to him from the shadowed corner. Putting a hand on the man's shoulder, he dropped his head and spoke. "Why did you try to knock Jackal out?"

"He talks too much. If he talks too much here, I'm sure he's doing the same out in the streets. So he got a sound check."

"Sound check?"

"Had to turn down his volume."

Adonis smiled at him and patted his shoulder. Bezerk didn't smile back, but he hunched his shoulders and turned, then left out of the room, leaving Adonis to himself.

"Sound check!" Then Adonis laughed out loud, getting up and putting a large gun in his waistband.

Chapter Eleven

The streets were crawling with people on the corner Winter had scouted out. There were a couple of the drug pushers she recognized from watching for a couple days. She didn't see the guy who had hit her, but for some reason, she didn't really expect to. The one who seemed over him, his boss or supplier, was who she was looking for. Her guess was he would be the way in or at least lead to a bigger fish that would lead to the main shark.

Hours creeped by as Winter waited. Not wanting to draw attention to herself, she went into a few stores close by. Then she drove and parked on a pay lot. That way, she could walk around a bit more. Then she got the break she was waiting for. The guy who probably took out the street boss drove up. Not the same car but same type of car, old, basic, but as nice as any brand new ride. He stood close to his car, pacing back and forth, smoking and looking down at his phone. Looking at his finger movements, she could tell he wasn't web surfing or texting. Just tapping. Anyone walking by or loosely watching wouldn't be the wiser.

A young dude came by and tossed something In the back door window. The guy turned and paced the opposite direction. About a minute later, another man tossed in something. The movement was so smooth that if you weren't looking for it, you wouldn't have seen it. The guy paced opposite again, but after each toss, he held his finger down on the phone. This went on for about five minutes. The guy put out his cigarette and headed to his car.

"Now! Now is my opportunity. "

Putting a cup up to her lips, she walked quickly towards him. Before he could get off the sidewalk, she bumped into him.

"Yo, watch where the fu… hey, you look familiar. "

"Excuse me. Hey, it's the hero. Out here saving more helpless females?"

"You're the woman Snow, my associate, hit. Are you okay? " he asked, stepping back and looking her up and down. "From what I can see, you don't look helpless."

Running her fingers through her hair then taking a sip of the drink, she posed with a hand on her hip. "Is that right? Think so?"

"Shit! If everything on you ain't sexy, you sure as hell don't need it."

The man in front of her wasn't bad looking, but the smell of stale cigarettes mixed with a heavy smell of weed on top of cheap cologne was almost unbearable. But she needed to get in good with him, to commence with her revenge.

"You never came by The Silver Spoon. Ah, what was your name again, Ms. Exotic?"

Playing the irritated hood girl role, she snapped, "It wasn't Exotic. Winter, darling. Say it with me. WINTER."

As he said her name, the smell again slapped her in the face. Not being able to take much more, she tried to hurry this along.

"Is that invite still good?"

"As good as you are. Matter of fact, I'm on my way there now. Care to join me for an early evening drink?"

"It is early in the evening, but I think one small glass of something wouldn't hurt me. One drink, sir."

"Cool. Hop in, and we'll be on the way."

"Thanks, but I think I'll drive myself. I don't know you. Hell, I don't even know your name."

With a foot and leg in his car, he looked over the hood. "The streets call me Dragon."

"Well, what shall I call you?"

Getting all the way in, he said out the window, "Like you said, you don't know me."

"Okay, Mr. Dragon. I know where it is. I'll be ten minutes behind you."

Getting in her ride, Winter smirked, "Dragon! Lead me to your zoo friends."

Chapter Twelve

Silver Spoon was crowded as usual, with diners sitting at tables and booths that had black leather seats and black satin tablecloths. This wasn't a high dollar, exclusive restaurant. In fact, it just looked expensive. The menu wasn't filled with exotic meats and hard to pronounce entrees. The idea behind the eatery was to have an atmosphere of fine dining for people who would never be able to go to a true place like that. The waiters wore white tuxedo shirts, black slacks and their choice of designer vests. The waitresses also wore white shirts and long black skirts, but they had their own choice of designer half-cut aprons. Full bar and hip-hop jazz played softly. The place was a hit with the neighborhood, and the owners, The Zoo Clan, made sure no trouble ever came to the area.

Winter stepped in and was immediately impressed. She had no idea how ordinary the dining was inside. Everything about the look of the restaurant, inside and out, said platinum or black card only.

Sitting in a booth way back in a shadowy corner, sat Dragon and some other men. As she walked over, he noticed her and motioned for her to come to them.

"Yo, Dragon, who this bitch?"

"Mommy thick as a frozen candy bar. This yours?"

Dragon blew smoke in the direction of the rude men in his presence. "Show some fucking respect! This is the woman I told y'all about. The one who caused Snowman to get melted." Then he took another pull off his weed-filled cigar.

Jackal got up and approached Winter. He walked a circle around her, then smacked her on the ass, saying, "If she ain't yours, I may have to claim all this ass for myself."

Just as Winter was about to slap him, the other guy quickly got up and came over.

"Fuck that!" Volcano pushed Jackal away. "Know your place before you get burnt." Then he flashed his gun that was sitting in his waistband. Turning back to Winter, he said, " What up, yo? What yo name? I got some special heat for you," while grabbing at his crotch.

"First of all, I don't want either of you—"

From out of a door in the back, a huge man walked up slowly. It seemed like the floor vibrated with every step he took.

Dragon spoke again through a cloud of smoke. "You two dumb motherfuckers. See what y'all done now. Here comes Bear." Then he slid over in the booth, making sure to be out of the way.

The big man was at least 6 '9" or maybe even 7' tall. Every bit 360 pounds of solid muscle. Coffee-colored skin, with a white, short beard. He grabbed Jackal, picked him off the ground and tossed him to the side like a child tossing a teddy bear.

Volcano raised his shirt and spoke in a shaky voice. "Now, Bear! Don't make me light you up with this torch." With speed faster than a blink, Bear had taken his gun and held it in his massive paws. Then, incredibly, he began to bend the gun in half and dropped it to the ground.

With a low growl, he spoke directly in Volcano's face. "If you ever make me come down here for some stupid shit again, or if you ever threaten me with something smaller than a bazooka, I will twist your spin like a pretzel. Are we clear or—"

Volcano swallowed hard. "We clear, Bear. We cool, man, you know my hot temper."

"Dead men are very cold. Remember that." Then he looked in Winter's direction. Nothing was said, but she knew his look asked 'are you good?'.

She said, "Everything is cool."

Bear adjusted his suit coat and nodded then went back through the door in back.

Chapter Thirteen

Sitting with the men trying to be social, but also trying to smoothly get information out of them, Winter wondered who was really in charge. Volcano was too easily irritated to be any kind of leader. Anything could set him off the deep end, but he kept it in check, not wanting to see Bear again. Dragon was top dog out of these three, but he was no leader, either. Jackal... Jackal had a mouthpiece on him, so if she was going to learn anything, it would be from him.

After a couple of hours and a few well-worded questions, Winter was slowly getting info out of the thugs. When she brought up the question of if Dragon was a good leader, Jackal spoke up.

"Dragon? Fuck no! He just like us. The main man is—"

"Told you, stop running that fucking mouth of yours." A fist flashed before everyone's eyes, knocking Jackal over into Volcano's lap.

"What in the entire shit is up with you, man?" Then Volcano looked at the man who threw the punch. Not another word was said.

Even Dragon looked a little nervous, which was shocking to Winter. Since she started keeping an eye on him, he had only shown two emotions—iceberg chill and beware of danger anger. Dropping his blunt and quickly picking it back up, Dragon's voice cracked as he spoke. "Damn, Bezerk! I think you may have broken his jaw."

Still looking at Jackal laid out in the booth, the man spoke with such a sinister tone, it sent chills down Winter's back. "He has been told to keep his mouth closed. Now, it will be closed for the next six to eight weeks."

Bezerk stood with his fist still balled and looked into everyone's eyes. Seemingly out of nowhere, another man appeared.

"See, if I was—"

"Don't start that 'if I was a bigger boss shit,' Serpent! You are what you are because no one can depend on you. Remember?"

"Yeah, but if I was in Dragon's spot, this punk ass here would have been dealt with a long time ago."

Dragon and Volcano got up and stepped towards Serpent. Dragon just blew smoke in his face while Volcano tapped the gun at his waist. Serpent backed up behind Bezerk and mumbled, "I was just saying."

Bezerk looked at Winter and asked who she was.

"That's the chick Snowman put hands on out in public. I asked her here as an apology for his actions."

"I'm sorry, Dragon. I don't believe I asked you a motherfucking thing! I asked this bitch." He was pointing at Winter but looking Dragon in the eyes, like he was burning his soul.

"My name is Winter. Not Bitch."

He squinted his eyes and gave her the meanest glare. "Whatever. It's time for you to go." Then he snapped his fingers and pointed towards the exit. Serpent was the first to start walking out. Volcano looked Winter up and down from behind and grinned, then he, too, left. Dragon nodded at Jackal, still slumped over in the booth.

Just then, the back door opened again and Bear emerged. Looking at Jackal, then Bezerk, he tilted his head and twisted his lips. Bezerk looked up at the man and frowned.

With that low, booming voice again, he asked, "More of your handiwork?"

"Don't start with me, Bear. You know how Jackal is. You want some too?"

Bear looked down at him, giving him a silent answer, 'like you know better.' Then he took up the sleeping man over one shoulder and looked at Winter.

"I'm still good. Thank you, Mr. Bear."

"Just Bear, Ms." Before leaving, he stopped and turned his head to look at Bezerk.

The smaller man announced, "You lucky I have to go, or I'd make a rug out of your big ass."

Bear moved a foot between Bezerk's feet and pressed down. To Winter's amazement, it sounded like the floor cracked under the pressure of that simple move. Bezerk turned and eyed Winter, looking at her like he was studying her. Then he, too, left.

Dragon was the last to leave, but before he did, he said to her, "Sorry, ma, things didn't go as planned, but I hope we are square now."

Picking up her drink and finishing it off, she replied, "We good. Thank you for the invite."

Dragon then took another pull off his blunt, nodded and walked out. Winter left seconds after him, behind a small group of women leaving out. Standing in a corner, she saw the four men get in their cars and trucks and leave. She now knew most of, if not all, the major players. Except for the head shot caller. It didn't matter. Once she started taking them out, he would reveal himself sooner or later, and unknowingly, Bear would be an assistant.

Chapter Fourteen

A few days has passed, and Winter paced the floor of the bedroom while she thought about how she was going to go about taking apart and taking down The Zoo Crew. Going after them one at a time wouldn't be a smart move. Any of them would kill her if she got too close or too nosey. Especially that Bezerk character. Dragon might be the most sensible one, but she knew that either he killed or ordered that corner man, Snowman, to be killed, so he was a no-go too. Serpent just seemed like his name sake, a snake, very sneaky. It was clear he wanted more than he was allowed to have. Maybe she could exploit that at some point. Now, Jackal... his lips were very loose, but for now, he wouldn't be saying much.

The doorbell rang and Winter jumped. Not expecting anyone this late in the evening, she went to open it. Stopping short and looking at the door, her mind asked her what Stephon would tell her to do. She went over to the couch and pulled out a small revolver tucked away in the cushions.

"Who is it?"

"It's Rob, Winter."

Letting her head fall back and exhaling a deep breath, she put the gun back and opened the door.

Rob walked in and gave her a light hug. She offered him a drink and asked where Grace was.

He replied, "She's home, getting dinner ready. I called to tell her I was stopping by to check on you."

"That is so sweet of you, Rob, but I'm fine."

Rob stood in the middle of the living room and gave Winter a questioning look. "Are you sure? Doran came by, right?"

"Yes, he did. Like you, he wanted to see how I was doing."

"Oh, good, and don't worry. Even though he said the case was suspended, I'm going to follow up on my own and find out who killed Stephon and who ordered it done."

She thought to herself, *that is if I don't get to them first.* "Thank you, Rob. I'm not completely sure what it is y'all do, or did, but I'll let you do what it is you do."

Rob gave her another hug and reassured her that she could trust him to take care of everything. Winter closed the door behind him when he left, then went back to her mental planning of how she would take out The Zoo.

Chapter Fifteen

———— ⚓ ⚓ ————

Adonis sat in his chair down in the basement of The Zoo layer. His irritation was obvious. He gripped the arm rests of his chair so hard, the wood was beginning to crack. His eyes met Dragon's and caused him to choked on the smoke in his lungs. Then he eyed Serpent, causing him to slide down in his chair like a child in trouble. Volcano tried to stand tough when his glance was met. Adonis started to pull himself up, making Cano sit his ass down. Next, was Bezerk. Adonis looked at him and gave a disappointed look. Taking a deep breath and closing his eyes, he knew Adonis was pissed but still had respect for him.

With more of a growl than an actual speech tone, Adonis spoke to the Zoo. "Can someone tell me exactly what the fuck is going on with y'all? Getting rid of a profitable corner man in the streets. Acting complete asses in Silver Spoon!" Adonis sat back in his huge chair, looking straight up in the air. "Answers, anyone?"

No one wanted to answer, knowing they could be the target of his rage. They all squirmed in their seats, waiting for each other to speak.

Being the low-down varmint he was, Jackal blurted out, "Dragon started all this shit, by killing Snowman.

Then he brought some bitch to The Spoon during a meeting."

Dragon damn near dropped his blunt, trying to get up out of his seat. "Punk ass bitch boy. Who the fuck are you to question what I do? That was a business decision and Adonis knows all about it and the woman was... fuck you. Why am I explaining my actions to you?"

Jackal retreated back in his seat like a wounded puppy. Adonis sat up and looked at Dragon. "Why was this woman at a meeting?"

"She wasn't at the meeting, actually. She was invited to the place as an apology for how Snowman treated her. She was going to be treated to a nice meal paid for by me. She just so happened to see me with the others in the back corner. Then some of these dumbasses were all over her, like a waitress in the strip club."

"I see. Good call on that, Drag. Defuse an issue before it becomes a problem. Now, he was trying to solve a problem, but I hear now, a few of you were causing more."

Bezerk spoke up. "It got handled. Volcano just needed time to cool down, and Jackal needed a nap."

Volcano giggled when he thought about Jackal getting knocked out.

Serpent asked, "Who handled it? I see both of them here, so it must not have been Bezerk!"

"Zerk put Jackal down, but Bear ended everything," Dragon said, lighting another blunt.

Adonis tapped his fingers on the armrest. "Y'all made Bear come break shit up?"

"It was handled! He didn't need to bring his big ass out there," Bezerk said in an irritated voice.

"Okay, I've heard enough. She sounds harmless, but make sure she isn't another undercover piece of shit like that guy we just eliminated. Volcano, I want you and Serpent to find and follow this chick. If you see anything suspicious, snatch her and bring her to me. Drag, I need you to go with Jackal and make sure he apologizes to Bear."

"For what?!"

"Because I said so. Bear is someone none of us wants a problem with."

A short time later, Dragon and Jackal arrived at The Silver Spoon. They asked one of the waiters to go and get Bear from the back. Jackal started arguing with Dragon about how unnecessary this was and that Bear could go to Hell. He wasn't going to tell him nothing. Dragon just blew smoke in his face and kept his eyes on the door in the back.

"Dragon, you ain't shit, and neither is Bear. Don't make me bust your ass."

"Jack, shut the fuck up before your ass bounces a check your wrote."

Jackal walked closer and put his finger in Drag's face. Drag pushed him back a few steps, causing Jackal to stumble. Embarrassed his bluff was called, he reached in his waistband to pull a gun. Just then, a huge hand grabbed his arm, stopping it from moving. Looking over his shoulder, he saw the shadow of a huge man. Then, by that same arm, he was picked up off the ground at least a foot.

"I heard you gentlemen wanted to see me, but it seems you're only here for trouble again. So please leave."

Putting out his blunt with the bottom of his shoe, Dragon spoke softly. "We meant no disrespect, Bear. Well, I didn't anyway. Jackal here wanted to apologize for the other night; ain't that right, Jackal?"

"Hell no! If he don't put me down, I'm going to knock him—"

Still holding the one arm, Bear flung him out like a towel. A grown human man, snapped in midair like a wet towel by a man... one-handed! After he straightened out, Jackal found himself still being held a foot off the ground, but now eye to eye with Bear, and his eyes were turning fire red.

"Bear! My bad, I meant no disrespect, man. Please accept my sincere apology."

Dragon laughed under his breath, but he made sure that Bear didn't see it. Bear then let Jackal go and turned his back. Without turning around, he said in that deep voice, "Accepted, just get out. Tell Adonis to control his kids, Dragon. This is his only courtesy warning."

Chapter Sixteen

Winter drove down a street, playing out different ways to get inside the Zoo's organization in her head. She thought of going through Dragon. He was very street smart but didn't have the ambition or heart to stand up to whoever was in charge. The one they called Cano or Volcano had the fury to do something. Probably nothing that could be useful. That loud mouth, Jackal, was a straight asshole and dumbass. He would be useful. She tapped on the steering wheel and nodded her head to the music. "The loud mouth it is."

Right behind her, in a dented up Chevy Nova, were Serpent and Volcano. The two happened to see the woman drive by, leaving a fish joint while they were trying to get with a couple of sexy women nearby. As they followed her, they argued like teenage girls. Volcano threatened to beat his ass and Serpent responded with a few foul words but planned on telling Adonis how he was messing the tailing mission up.

"You too fucking close, man. She going to spot us!"

"Calm down! I got this. It's not the first time I had to follow a bitch."

"Pull over and let me drive, motherfucker."

"Sit back and cool out, Cano. Damn."

Volcano put his finger against Serpent's head and pushed it, causing it to bounce off the window. Furious, Serpent turned to look at Volcano and tried to punch him. While cussing and swinging on each other, they crashed right into the back of the SUV in front of them. They stopped fighting but continued to curse each other.

The SUV they hit rolled to a stop against the curb. The driver stumbled out and looked at the damage, then to the vehicle that had caused it. Straining to focus, looking through blurred vision, the faces in the other vehicle were somewhat familiar.

Holding her head with one hand and the other hand on the side of her wrecked SUV, Winter looked into the car, past the folded up hood and cracked windshield.

"Oh, shit!! They followed me. Do they know who I am? Were they sent to kill me?" She turned and tried to run but bounced off everything around, trying to get away.

Falling out of the wrecked old school, the two thugs pointed fingers at each other, blaming the other for causing the accident.

"Motherfucker, I'm going to tell Adonis you fucked up this whole thing."

Irritated, Volcano pulled out his gun and shot Serpent right in his mouth. "You won't be bumping your gums to Adonis or anyone else again, bitch!"

Serpent crawled around on the ground, gargling thick clots of blood, because the bullet came directly out the back of his neck, missing the lower part of his brainstem. Volcano stood over him and put seven more bullets in him, from his head, down his back, to his butt. He looked around at the people watching in horror. Spotting the woman trying to get away, he began firing into the crowd, not giving a damn. All they had to do was follow this bitch, but Serpent messed that up.

Winter heard the gun firing behind her and the sounds of people yelling and screaming. Bodies started dropping around her as she regained her focus and balance. Breaking into a run, she went around a building. While she hid in a doorway, she pulled out her gun and tried pulling in her curvaceous body as much as possible. One after the other, people ran by her, not even seeing her in the shadow of the doorway. Then the sound of someone cussing frantically got louder.

"Fuck! Fuck! Stupid bitch! Where the hell did you go?"

Slowing to look through the crowd ahead of him, Volcano began to walk and reload his gun. Knowing the police were on their way, he had to kill this chick now! He could make up some story to tell Adonis later. Cursing loudly one more time, he looked over at the shadowy doorway to see a gun pointed at him. He blinked and frowned, then he never did another thing again.

Winter put her gun away, stepping over the body, and ran back to her ride to tell the police she was hit then hid because the two men had started shooting.

As she waited, she thought, *two down, more to go.*

Chapter Seventeen

Adonis paced around and around his chair, with his head up, breathing hard and loud. There were a few men sitting in chairs around the room who were way too scared to move or say anything. With each pass by of the chair, Adonis looked each man in his eyes. He picked up a gun clip and threw it at a wall behind Jackal, causing him to fall over out of his chair. Looking over his shoulder from the floor, Jackal saw the clip stuck in the wall from the force of Adonis' throw.

"Get up, you punk son-of-a-bitch! If I wanted to take you out, I would have grabbed your head and pulled your brain out!"

Jackal got up and sat back down, leaving a small puddle of pee on the ground. Dragon shifted in his seat, bracing for whatever. Bezerk leaned against the wall, stone-faced as usual, but inside, he, too, was a little nervous. He would never show any kind of fear, but he knew his crazy was no match for the fury and strength of Adonis.

"Who is this bitch? She blasted Serpent and Volcano, then just vanished in the crowd? How in the fuck could this be? Dragon, I put this on you. I lost two animals to her. This is on your head, and if one of you motherfuckers don't kill this bitch, I'm going to start killing. Understand? Am I clear?"

He picked up a custom-made three barrel pump shotgun and pointed it at all of them. "Now, get the hell out of here!"

The nervous men got up and quickly got out of his sight. Bezerk eased out, as well, but kept up his tough guy appearance. From out of the shadows behind the huge chair, a man in a suit came into the light. The man walked past Adonis and was about to speak until he was shoved into a chair. Grabbing the arm rests, he looked up in shock, then a large boot said hello to his chest, causing the chair he was in to slide about seven feet back. His heart thumped fast and hard, so much so, his shirt was moving around it. When the shotgun was placed in his face, his heart completely stopped.

"What the hell am I paying you for? This bitch has to be an undercover or government something! You are supposed to give me a heads up or eliminate shit like this!"

With a shaky voice, the man answered, "I don't know who she is, Adonis. I haven't even seen the woman."

"Well, that will be taken care of soon. When they bring her in or drag her body in, you can tell me who she is then."

"You know I can't be seen with you, man."

"You will do what the fuck I tell you to do, or should I keep my cash and find a new connect?"

"Nah, man. You still need me."

Pushing the barrel against his temple, Adonis asked, "You say I NEED you?"

"I mean, I'm still useful."

"We shall see. Now, get out until I tell you to come and eye this chick."

After the guy left, Adonis got on his cellphone and called Bezerk, telling him put the word out that he wanted her alive, so he could ask her some questions. He had to stress that fact a couple of times, but his point was made. Hanging up, he said to himself, "Tick-tock, bitch. Your life is on the clock now."

Chapter Eighteen

An empty glass with half-melted ice touched the table again, only to be picked right back up and refilled. Before emptying the glass for the fourth time, she placed it against her forehead so the cool glass could ease a bumping pressure. Winter took the alcohol-filled glass and once again swallowed the contents. She never thought that she would have to kill anyone, but she had found it rather easy. It could have come from the fact that it was life or death—pulling the trigger on someone trying to take her out wasn't hard. Stephon had prepared her well. Prepared her for a situation just like this. How did he know she would need to know how to—

Then she realized he was undercover and he'd figured, at some point, his cover might be blown and she would have to know how to protect herself if someone came for them, or her only.

There was a knock at the door that caused Winter to jump. Immediately, she snatched up one of the blue guns. She didn't answer, just slowly walked up and peeked out the side of the window, then smiled when the person outside the door leaned back and gave her the middle finger.

As she came in the door, Grace asked, "Girl, where have you been? Rob and I have been worried sick." Then she hugged her friend.

"Grace, I've been so busy. I'm sorry I haven't been in contact, but I'm good."

"Obviously not," she replied, looking down at the gun, "and don't give me that cleaning it shit. What's really going on?"

"Okay, okay. I'll fill you in, but I'm going to need another bottle cause you're going to need a drink after hearing this shit."

"All right. Guess I'll drive, cause I don't see your ride."

"I was in an accident, and it kind of got shot up."

"Shot up! To hell with a drink. I'm going to need some weed for this sit down. Come on, Dirty Harriet, put up the gun so we can ride out."

The women picked up their alcohol and stopped by Grace's home for some smoke medication before going back to Winter's. As they rode and sang with the radio loudly with the windows down, they were passed by a car with two young men in it.

"Bingo! There goes that bitch, there in that green drop top."

Dragon blew a huge cloud of smoke out the passenger window. "Bust that U-turn and we'll snatch them up." Jackal smiled, turned the old school Chevelle around and followed.

Stopping at an intersection, the women paid no attention to the two men walking up on both sides. A black bag was placed on both of their heads, followed by punches to the face, knocking each unconscious.

Pulling out his cellphone, Dragon made the call. "Yo, Adonis, mission accomplished. We got her."

"Bring her in. Now!"

"We got a bonus. She was with another thick chick. Might be able to use her somewhere."

"I'll see when you get here, and well done, Drag. That's why you only get the hard talk. I know you'll eventually come through. Come on in. I need to make a call."

Adonis punched in a preset number, and when the call was answered, he only said, "Time to identify the body. Get here in twenty minutes, or you'll be dead in thirty." Then he hit end.

Chapter Nineteen

Winter woke up in a haze, tied to a chair with a bag or sack over her head. To her right, she could hear Grace calling her name. Trying to figure out where she was and what the hell happened to her... to them... she didn't answer Grace right away. Winter wanted to see if there was anyone else in the area with them. She blocked out Grace's calls and listened for other breathing or echoing movements. Stephon had taught her how to quiet her mind and focus on different sounds around herself. Satisfied they were alone, she answered Grace. "Yes, Grace, I'm here, and from what I can tell, we are alone, for now."

"Why are we here? Who did this to us? What are they going to do to us?"

"We will be all right for now. If they wanted to kill us right away, we would've been taken out in the car. We are about to be questioned."

"By whom, Winter?"

"My guess is the leader of the gang called the Zoo. Adonis."

The creaking of a door opening drew the attention of the two women. They both turned their heads in the direction of the sound. Unable to see, they still looked towards the sound. They heard the sound of footsteps. Then another set, and another set, followed by heavy, purposeful steps. Mumbling between some men, then the blinding lights overhead caused Winter and Grace to squint their eyes after the bags were removed.

"Well, well, well. Which one of these pretty ladies killed two of my men? Was it you, honey?" He slapped Grace hard across her face. "Or was it this thick bitch?" he asked, fondling Winter's breasts. "Damn, is this blue hair for real, or a wig?" He got closer to examine her hair. "I'll be damned. It's black but looks blue!"

Dragon lit up and blew an aroma-filled cloud of smoke. "That's the one."

Jackal came over and put his hands on her lips. "Let's see what these full lips can do."

Adonis grabbed him by the back of his shirt and tossed him against the wall. "Go sit the fuck down, before I put you down for good."

"If blue hair is our troublemaker, who is this little piece of thick ass?"

Grace looked up at Adonis and into his hypnotic brown eyes. He wore a dark-green tank top that caressed his body, showing every muscle on the upper half of his body. Camouflage pants hung over tree trunk-sized thighs. The smell of his cologne on any other day, any other place, would have made her cookie bang like a drum, but being tied to a chair killed that vibe.

"Please don't hurt us! We don't know why we are here, but I'm sure it's a mistake."

"Not a mistake. Just unfortunate for you. She is supposed to be here. You are just an extra fly in the web. She killed two of my men."

"No, I killed one, and that was after he shot the other."

"Bullshit," Jackal said from over on the wall where he had been thrown.

Winter looked at Adonis with an icy glare. In her mind, she was telling herself that this was the man who'd ordered the hit on Stephon. Finally, the monster at the center of the Zoo. She sized him up for a weakness. He was built to perfection. Clearly, he was one of those people who got stronger when angered. Dangerous, because he had superhuman strength already.

"They rammed the back of my SUV, causing both of us to crash. One got out yelling at the other, then he pulled out a gun and shot him. He came running after me, shooting through a crowd. In self-defense, yes, I shot and killed him."

"Dumbasses!" Adonis growled before he picked up an empty chair and destroyed it on the floor. "Had to be that hothead Volcano blasting recklessly. Stupid moves get stupid results."

Bezerk came in and whispered something in Adonis' ear.

"About damn time! Bring him in."

Bezerk opened a door, allowing a slim-built man to come in. Winter and Grace both looked at the man walking in and dropped their jaws.

"Grace? Winter? What the fuck are you two doing here?"

Chapter Twenty

If an alien holding a bright red-bladed machete had roller skated into the room, the women wouldn't have been more surprised. Never in three million years, would they have ever guessed this man would... could...

"Now that I have our mystery woman in front of us, would you please come over here and identify this bitch."

"Yes, I know her. I... know both of them." He walked over and stood in front of the women with sadness in his eyes. "This is Mrs. Winter Topp. She is the wife of Stephon Topp, the agent who infiltrated your organization."

Adonis walked over and glared in her face. Without looking in his direction, he asked Bezerk, "I thought you told me everyone in the room was eliminated."

"She was bleeding so bad, I just knew the double barrel had hit her too."

Walking away from the women and standing next to Bezerk, he quietly said to him, "You made a mistake on this. Since this is your first time doing so and you have never disappointed me before, I will just give you a warning. Don't let shit like this happen again."

Turning back to the women, he stood in front of them again, with hands behind his back. "So, we know who you are and why you are here, but who are you, mystery lady number two?"

The man behind Adonis spoke. "That is Grace. Grace is my wife."

Adonis looked over his shoulder and growled, "Your wife?" He turned back to see the hurt and anger mixed in her eyes. "So I see you didn't know your husband Rob was on my payroll as informant, or a rat, if you will." Then he looked at Winter. "How do you think we found out about your man? Rob gave us a heads up and told us where to find him and you. He just didn't give us much detail on you, just that he was married to chick built like a fine brick house. Only, if he'd mentioned the hair color, you would have been made immediately."

"I didn't know you were going to kill him. You said you were just going to hurt him! You didn't say anything about murder or hurting Winter!"

"Don't try to make yourself a victim here! You gladly took my money for the information."

Rob shoved Adonis to the side and kneeled in front of Grace. "I am so sorry you got dragged into this. It was only supposed to be them. You were never supposed to know about—"

Just then, Rob's head and part of his upper body exploded into Grace's face. Adonis lowered the huge gun he had just pointed behind Rob. "That was for pushing me, you worthless piece of dog shit. Bezerk! Time to redeem yourself. Do it right this time."

Bezerk nodded his head and smiled as he walked over to the middle of the room. At that moment, the door to the small room opened as Joe stepped in, followed by Bear.

Chapter Twenty-One

———◦ ◦———

Bear had come to see Adonis and confront him about his lackeys, but when he saw the two women tied up and the headless body lying in front of him, his blood began to heat up. Bear didn't bother to ask what was going on; he went over to the ladies to untie them. Everyone knew Bear was a big, tough guy and not the kind of person that you would want to have mad at you. The broken bodies that were left in his huge shadow were countless. Something no one knew was that Bear had a soft spot for women, but only good women in trouble. Good women like Winter. From the first meeting, he could tell she wasn't the type to hang around this type of crew unless there was a purpose.

"Bear, this is none of your business. If you would kindly give us a moment in here, I will attend to whatever business you are here for."

The giant man paused and moved toward Adonis. Bezerk slowly moved between the two men. Joe also closed in on him.

"Why are these ladies bound, Adonis? What kind of man does this? Even if you are interrogating them for information, a man of your size shouldn't have to result to this method. Let alone having a room full of backup."

Winter yelled out, "Bear, they murdered my husband in our house, right in front of me. That body was her husband. That is his blood and part of his head on our faces."

Bezerk ran over and punched Winter right in the mouth. "Shut up, bitch! I should have blown your blue-haired head off like I did your husband!"

Looking up at Bezerk, Winter said, "So it was you who pulled the trigger!"

Before he could answer, he was off the ground and flying through the air. Bear had grabbed him by a shoulder and the waistband, throwing him several feet across the room, against a wall. Adonis rushed in from behind, hitting Bear in the back of the head with the gun he held. Bear stumbled forward only one step, slightly bending at the knee. Adonis was amazed as he lifted the weapon to see it was now bent, rendering its shooting capability useless.

"Ladies, I am sorry about this, but there is no time for nothing else." Bear grabbed the two chairs in either hand, and with a violent yank, he smashed the chairs together, turning the wooden seats into splinters and setting the women free.

With all the loud commotion, Dragon and Jackal rushed in to the fight from the back of the room just as Adonis was throwing wild, hard punches to Bear, having little effect. The two lackeys looked at each other, knowing fighting Bear would be like going against a living T-Rex. They both shrugged their shoulders and went in to help their boss.

Joe ran at Bear and was greeted with a thunderous punch to the heart, killing him instantly.

Grace slid back against the wall and watched as Winter got up and ran to her purse that was sitting in an opposite corner. Jackal saw Winter moving away from the ruckus and decided to take her on instead of the angry giant. Winter slid across the floor as she dove for her purse. Jackal reached for her legs, but he was met with blue steel pointing at his head. The flame from the barrel was the last thing he saw in life.

Adonis, Dragon, Bezerk and Bear turned to where the shot came from. They saw Jackal dead on the floor and Winter holding a smoking gun. Adonis threw his broken weapon at Winter, striking her in the arm and causing her to fire a shot into the ceiling. Dragon rushed over and kicked her in the face. She dropped the gun and fell back. Bear punched Adonis in the back, making the built, but smaller, man fall to his knees.

"Big motherfucker!" Bezerk yelled, picking up a piece of one of the broken chairs and striking Bear in the head. The wild assault was actually working. When Bear turned around, he had received a direct blow across the eyes and bridge of the nose. With a roar, the big man finally fell, holding his face. Bezerk stood over the man and came down on his head with a blow that would have split a log.

Dragon picked Winter up and tried to drag her over to Adonis, who was getting up. "Bring that bitch to me. I'm going to crush her head like an egg."

Grace finally made a move after staring at Rob's headless body. She picked up a long, jagged piece of wood and ran it through the back of Bezerk's knee. His scream distracted Dragon and Adonis, so Winter picked her gun back up off the ground and gave Dragon several bullets to the back and side. Then she sent two bullets into the right side of Adonis' chest.

Now, both men lay on the ground, cussing and rolling around. Winter got up and went back to her purse. Taking out her other gun, she tossed it over to Grace.

"We both got scores to settle. I know how I'm going to do mine. How you do yours is completely on you."

At the same time, both women started walking. Passing each other in the middle of the room, they stood over the murderers of their husbands. Winter checked the bullets left in her clip as Grace chambered a bullet in her gun.

Grace kicked Adonis a few times until he turned to face her.

"What's wrong, honey, can't accept the truth that your husband was a rat and got your friend's husband murked?"

"I accept the fact I will spend the rest of my life making it right with her, and you will spend the rest of your life watching a bullet enter your eye." Then she pulled the trigger and put one through his eye and into his head.

Winter stood over Bezerk and stepped on his fingers, breaking them. "Was that the hand you used to pull the trigger on Stephon? Or was it the other hand?" Then she stomped on the other one.

Both hands now had multiple broken fingers, so using a gun would be impossible. A long piece of wood was still going through his right knee, so running was out of the question. Dragon, Jackal, Joe and his boss Adonis were all dead, and Bear lay on the floor from a board to the head from him. He knew he only had one choice left.

"Please don't kill me. I was only following orders. Adonis threatened our lives constantly if we didn't do as he commanded. I never wanted to hurt anyone. Oh God, please forgive me. Please God, don't kill me."

Winter kneeled down and gave him the look a mother would give a hurt child. Then she gave him a kiss on the forehead. For some odd reason, her lips were as cold as the night air in mid-January. The coldness from a person who had no heart.

Standing up, she said, "God can't hear you right now, but you can tell him your pleas in person." Then she emptied her gun in his face, bringing her justice for her beloved Stephon. The two women nodded at each other and started walking out as Winter made a call after retrieving her purse.

Reaching up, Bear grabbed their hands as they passed him lying on the floor. Stopping, they both helped him sit up. Excited their helper was still alive, they looked him over.

"Thank you. Are you ladies all right?"

"We should be asking you that."

"I will be fine after a while. Right now, my head is splitting." He laughed as he wiped the blood from his forehead. The women giggled also, then helped him to his feet. With arms over their shoulders, the three left the dead to tend for themselves.

Epilogue

Dorian sat across from Winter in her home, as they discussed the elimination of The Zoo Gang. He told her he was scared there was a snake in his grass, but he couldn't weed him out. He apologized several times that he couldn't find him sooner, to save Stephon.

"What you did was careless, dangerous and completely stupid, but what you did with the little training you were given by your husband was impressive."

"Thank you. I was trained pretty well, but this was something I needed to do. Something I needed to settle."

"Winter, I lost a very good agent, but I think I know of a competent replacement for him."

"Already? Hope this new guy does well for you."

"Well, if the offer is accepted, I believe *she* would do very well."

"She?"

"Yes. She. I would like you to take your husband's position in the agency."

"But I—"

"You would do just fine. With a bit more training, that is. What do you say?"

Winter sat back in her chair and just looked at him. Then she smiled. "When do we get started?"

The End

About the Author

A lifelong resident of Louisville, Kentucky, this author has cultivated a passion for storytelling since adolescence. Now published through Royal Media and Publishing, the author has penned eight captivating urban fiction and mystery thriller novels. Known for crafting concise narratives that maintain reader engagement with each chapter, their works span several genres within urban fiction and mystery thriller categories.

Find Michael Young's books on Amazon.com, www.royalmediastore.com and at Pretty Woman Boutique.

To connect with Michael Young, find him on social media:

Facebook @ michael.young.5680899

IG @ mrbigmike1972

More Books by Michael Young

The
Dark Side
of **DESIRE**

MICHAEL A. YOUNG